MERCER MAYER'S LITTLE MONSTER® PRIVATE EYE™ THE LOST WISH

To Charlie VanKirk

Written by Erica Farber and J.R. Sansevere

A Mercer Mayer Ltd. / J.R. Sansevere Book

 Published in the United States by Inchworm Press, an imprint of GT Publishing Corporation,
16 East 40th Street, New York, New York 10016.
Printed in China.

Allow me to introduce myself.
My name is Little Monster Private Eye.

This is my trusty assistant Detective Kerploppus. Together we do our best to keep law and order in Monsterville.

One morning my best friend, Jerry Bombanant, came to our office with his little brother, Larry. They had a case for us to solve. Larry had lost his lucky green coin.
LITTLE MONSTER PRIVATE EYE

“Little Monster, it’s time for lunch!” called my mother.
“Care to join me?” I said. “We can discuss the case over lunch.”

Larry stopped crying long enough to eat three peanut-butter and pickle sandwiches.

"When did you lose your lucky green coin?" I asked him.

"This morning at the fountain when I went to make my birthday wish," Larry said.

"To the fountain!" I said. "On the double!"

S
P

Detective Kerploppus and I hopped into
the Private Eye Mobile and sped toward
the fountain.
Jerry and Larry followed close behind.
Is that a parade?

Looks like Little Monster Private Eye is on a case!
You shouldn't play in the road.

Detective Kerploppus and I inspected the scene of the crime.
"No green coins here!" said Detective Kerploppus.
Then I questioned Larry.
"When you left the house this morning,
how many coins did you have?" I asked.
"Three," said Larry.

“How many coins do you have now?” I asked.
“One,” said Larry.
He pulled it out of his pocket.
There was not a spot of green on it.
“We’ll call this Coin Number One,” I said.

"What did you do with the other two coins?" I asked.
"I traded one for a marble with my friend Sam," said Larry.

We all headed for the basketball court where Sam was warming up for the big game.

"Little Monster Private Eye here," I said. "Detective Kerploppus and I would like to see the coin Larry traded with you."

Sam slam-dunked the ball.
"It was a fair trade," she said.

Then she pulled the coin out of her pocket.
There wasn't a spot of green on Coin Number Two either.
"That means that Coin Number Three must be Larry's lucky green coin," I said.

I asked Larry what he had done with Coin Number Three.
"I bought a piece of banana bubble gum at Mr. Whizzle's Candy Factory," said Larry.
"Next stop Mr. Whizzle's!" I said.
CLUE MAP
#1
#2
#3

All was quiet at the Candy Factory.

"Can I help you?" asked Mr. Whizzle.

I nodded. "Larry bought a piece of banana bubble gum from you this morning," I said. "And he paid for it with a very special green coin."

Mmm. Radish-flavored gum!
Whizzle CANDY

Mr. Whizzle opened the cash register.
Detective Kerploppus and I examined all the coins.
We were stumped! The lucky green coin wasn't there!

Suddenly, I had an idea. I asked Mr. Whizzle how many customers he had after Larry bought the bubble gum.

“Only one,” said Mr. Whizzle. “Mrs. Yalapappus. She bought a pound of jellybeans and I gave her some coins as change.”

“A-ha!” I said. “To Yalapappus Manor pronto!”

I told Mrs. Yalapappus we were looking for a lucky green coin we believed she might have gotten as change from Mr. Whizzle that morning.

"I keep all my coins in a jar," she said. "Follow me."

Guess what we found in the jar?
Coin Number Three—Larry's lucky green coin!
"Now I can make my birthday wish!" shouted Larry.
"Hooray!"

Detective Kerploppus and I went with Jerry and Larry to the fountain. We watched Larry throw in his lucky green coin and make his birthday wish.

Later that afternoon Detective Kerploppus and I went to Larry's birthday party.
We got there right before Grandpa Bombanat.
"Grandpa!" yelled Larry. "You're here! My birthday wish came true!"

Detective Kerploppus and I had cookies and cake to celebrate.
And so ended what we came to call the Case of the Lost Wish….